sleep-overs

I wonder if you've ever had a sleepover? How many people came? You can have a sleepover with just one special friend or you can have a big sleepover with lots of children camping in the living room with sleeping bags and pillows everywhere! Sleepovers can be great fun, chatting and giggling and eating and making stuff and painting fingernails and inventing new hairstyles and listening to your favourite music and watching DVDs. The only thing you don't seem to do on a sleepover is sleep! Sometimes you don't settle down till ten o'clock, eleven o'clock, twelve o'clock, even one o'clock. It's not a good idea to plan anything too energetic the next day!

I loved writing about the five special sleepovers in this book. It was great fun inventing a different theme for each party and describing all the presents and the birthday cakes. My main girl, Daisy, wants to have a sleepover party too – but she's also very worried. She's not sure how her new friends will react to her sister Lily, who has special needs. Emily will be fine, because she's such a sweet girl. Daisy would give anything to have Emily for her very best friend – but Emily's already got a best friend, Chloe. Chloe looks as if butter wouldn't melt in her mouth but she is seriously scary, and absolutely horrible to Daisy.

I think we've all known someone like Chloe! She's so mean in this book – but don't worry, something very unfortunate happens to her right at the end!

I hope all your sleepover parties are splendid affairs!

Jacqueline Wilson

sleep-overs

Jacqueline Wilson

Illustrated by Nick Sharratt

YOUNG CORGI

SLEEPOVERS
A YOUNG CORGI BOOK 978 0 552 55783 2

First published in Great Britain by Doubleday,
an imprint of Random House Children's Books
A Random House Group Company

Doubleday edition published 2001
First Young Corgi edition published 2002
This Young Corgi edition published 2008

5 7 9 10 8 6

The Random House Group Limited makes every effort to ensure that the papers used in its books
are made from trees that have been legally sourced from well-managed and credibly certified forests.
Our paper procurement policy can be found at: www.randomhouse.co.uk/paper.htm

Young Corgi Books are published by Random House Children's Books,
61–63 Uxbridge Road, London W5 5SA

www.kidsatrandomhouse.co.uk
www.rbooks.co.uk

Addresses for companies within The Random House Group Limited can be found at:
www.randomhouse.co.uk/offices.htm

THE RANDOM HOUSE GROUP Limited Reg. No. 954009

A CIP catalogue record for this book is available from the British Library.

Printed in the UK by CPI Bookmarque, Croydon, CR0 4TD

* One *

"Guess what!" said Amy. "It's my birthday next week and my mum says I can invite all my special friends for a sleepover party."

"Great," said Bella.

"Fantastic," said Chloe.

"Wonderful," said Emily.

I didn't say anything. I just smiled. Hopefully.

I wasn't sure if I was one of Amy's *special* friends. Amy and Bella were best friends. Chloe and Emily were best friends. I didn't have a best friend yet at this new school.

Well, it wasn't quite a new school, it was quite old, with winding stairs and long polished corridors and lots and lots of classrooms, some of them in Portakabins in the playground. I still got a bit lost sometimes. The very first day I couldn't find the girls' toilets and went hopping round all playtime, getting desperate. But then Emily found me and took me to the toilets herself. I liked Emily *sooooo* much. I wished she could be my best friend. But she already had Chloe for her best friend.

I didn't think much of Chloe.

I liked Amy and Bella though. We'd started to go round in a little bunch of five, Amy and Bella and Emily and Chloe and me. We formed this special secret club. We called ourselves the Alphabet Girls. It's because of our names. I'm Daisy. So our first names start with A B C D and E. I was the one who spotted this. The secret club was all my idea too.

I always wanted to be part of a special secret club. It was almost as good as having a best friend.

I wasn't sure if Amy's birthday sleepover was
strictly reserved for best friends only. Amy went on
talking and talking about her sleepover and how
she knew she wasn't going to sleep all night long.
Bella teased her because one time when Amy
spent the night at Bella's she fell sound asleep at
nine o'clock and didn't wake up till nine o'clock
the next morning. Chloe said she sometimes didn't
go to bed till ever so late, eleven or even twelve at
night, so she'd stay awake, no bother. Emily said
she always woke up early now because her new
baby brother started crying for his bottle at six
o'clock every single day.

I still didn't say anything. I tried to keep on smiling.

Emily looked at me. Then she looked at Amy. "Hey, Amy. Daisy can come too, can't she?"

"Of course," said Amy.

My mouth smiled until it almost tickled my ears. "Whoopee!" I yelled.

"Really, Daisy!" said Chloe, clutching her ears in an affected way. "You practically deafened me."

"Sorry," I said – though I wasn't. But you have to try to keep on the right side of Chloe. She's the one who tells everyone what to do. The Boss.

She even tried to tell Amy what to do at her own sleepover. "You've got to get some seriously scary videos, right?" she said.

"My mum won't let me watch *seriously* scary videos," said Amy.

"Don't tell your mum. Just wait till she's gone

8

to bed and then we can all watch in your bedroom," said Chloe, sighing because she thought it was so simple.

"I don't have a video recorder in my bedroom, just a portable television," said Amy.

"I haven't even got my own television," said Bella comfortingly. "Never mind. Hey, what are you going to have for your birthday tea, Amy?"

Bella likes food. She always has big bars of chocolate at break-time. She eats eight squares herself. She gives Amy three squares because she's her best friend, but she lets Chloe and Emily and me have one square each. Chloe sometimes gobbles the last square too. Chloe gets away with murder.

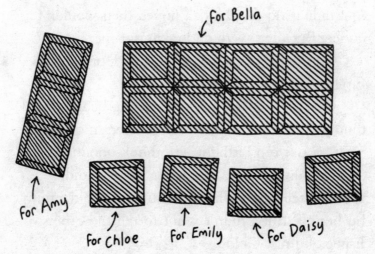

For Bella

For Amy

For Chloe

For Emily

For Daisy

"Mum says I can have a big birthday cake," said Amy. She smiled at Bella. "*Chocolate* cake!"

"No, have an iced cake in a special shape. They're seriously cool," said Chloe.

"Amy can have what she likes. It's her sleepover," said Bella.

Chloe frowned.

"We can *all* have sleepovers on our birthdays," said Emily quickly. "Then we can each choose the way we want them to be. If we're allowed. My mum's going nuts looking after my baby brother but I *think* she'll let me have a sleepover."

"Mine will too," said Bella.

"My mum lets me do anything I like," said Chloe. "So does my dad."

I didn't say anything. I hoped they wouldn't notice. But they were all looking at me.

"Can you have a sleepover too, Daisy?" said Emily.

"Oh sure," I said quickly, but my heart started thumping under my new school sweatshirt.

It wasn't my birthday *yet*, thank goodness.

I couldn't have a sleepover party. I didn't want to tell them why. I might have told Emily by herself. But I didn't want to tell the others. Especially not Chloe.

✴TWO✴

I told Mum about Amy's sleepover party while we were having tea.

"That's lovely, Daisy," she said, but I could tell she wasn't really listening. She was too busy concentrating on feeding my sister, Lily.

"There now, Lily, yum yum," Mum mumbled, spooning yoghurt into Lily's mouth. Mum's own mouth opened and shut. Lily's mouth didn't always open and shut at the right time. It snapped shut so the spoon clanked against her teeth, or suddenly gaped open so the yoghurt drooled down her chin.

Mum mopped at her. Lily's arm jerked up

and she tried to grab the cloth.

"There! Did you see that, Daisy? Lily's trying to wipe her own chin. *Clever* girl, Lily!"

"Mm, clever girl," I said.

My sister Lily isn't clever. She isn't my little baby sister. She isn't little at all. She's my big sister. She's eleven years old but she isn't in the top year at school. Lily doesn't go to my new school. She didn't go to my old school either. She never used to go to school at all, she just stayed at home with Mum, but now she goes to this new special school. That's why we moved, so that she could go there. It's a special school because Lily has special needs. That's the right way to describe her. There are lots and lots of *wrong* ways. Some children at my old school used to call Lily horrible names when they saw Mum pushing her in the street. They used to call me names too.

I don't think Emily would call Lily horrible names. Or Amy or Bella. But I'm not at all sure about Chloe.

I'd shut up about my sister Lily since I'd started to go to this new school. I didn't want anyone calling her names.

Though *I* call her names sometimes. I get mad at her. She isn't like a real sister. We can't play

12

together and swap clothes and dance and giggle
and mess about. She's not like a big sister because
she can't ever tell me stuff and hold my hand
across roads and watch out for me at school.
She's not like a little sister either because she's too
big to sit on my lap and she's too heavy for me to
carry around. It's even getting a struggle to push
her in her wheelchair.

Something went wrong with Lily when she
was born. She won't ever be able to walk or talk.
Well, that's what Dad says. Mum says we just
don't know. Dad says we do know, but Mum
won't face facts. Mum and Dad have rows about
Lily and I hate it. Sometimes I almost hate her
because she's always in the way and she cries a
lot and she wakes us all up in the night and she
takes up so much time. But I always feel lousy if
I'm mean to Lily. I get into her bed at night

when Mum and Dad are asleep and I whisper sorry in Lily's ear. I cuddle her. She doesn't exactly cuddle me back but she acts like she's glad I'm there. She makes these little soft sounds. I pretend it's Lily talking to me in her own secret language. I whisper secrets to her under the covers and she whispers "ur-ur-ur-ur-ur" back to me. It's as if we're having our own tiny private sleepover just for us.

I got into bed with her that night and told her all about Amy's sleepover. I've told her all about Amy and Bella. I've told her heaps about Emily and how I wish she could be my best friend. I've told her heaps about Chloe too and how I wish she didn't sometimes act like she was my worst enemy.

"What's that you're saying, Lily?" I whispered. "Oh, I get it! You say that Emily's probably going to get seriously fed up with Chloe being so mean and moody all the time. You think she's going to break friends with her and be *my* best friend instead?"

Lily went, "Ur ur ur ur ur."

I gave her a grateful hug. Sometimes I was almost glad she was my sister.

* Three *

Amy and Bella and Chloe and Emily and I all got very excited about the sleepover party. We talked about it all the time at school. We talked about it so much that our teacher Mrs Graham got cross with us.

She got especially cross with Chloe because her voice was the loudest. She kept her in at playtime. I had a lovely playtime with Emily. She said she liked my long hair and wished she could brush it, so I undid my plaits and then we played hairdressers and I was a posh lady going to a dance and Emily was fixing my hair for me, and she gave me a facial too, with soap from the washbasins in the girls' cloakrooms. I didn't wash all the soap off properly so my face felt a bit stiff

when we went into the classroom. It went stiffer still when I saw Chloe glaring at me. I knew she was going to get me.

"You mean pig, Daisy!" she yelled as soon as it was going-home time. "It was all *your* fault. *You* were saying something stupid about how you've never been to a sleepover before so *I* said you can't have had any friends at your old school and then Mrs Graham got cross with me when *I* didn't start saying stuff, it was *you*. Why didn't you tell her it was all your fault?"

"It wasn't really Daisy's *fault*," said Emily.

"Yes it was! She wouldn't own up. She let me take the blame. She's horrible. I don't know why we have to have her tagging around with us all the time," said Chloe.

"Don't be like that, Chloe," said Emily, putting her arm round her. "Here, do you want a chocolate biscuit? I saved it for you."

Chloe wouldn't take the chocolate biscuit so Bella ate it.

"Are you really having a chocolate cake for  your birthday, Amy?" said Bella.

"Yeah, my mum's friend's making it. And we're having egg sandwiches and sausages on sticks

16

and cheese and pineapple and fancy ice-creams and special fruity drinks with teeny umbrellas," said Amy, her eyes shining.

"Like grown-up cocktails," I said.

"Is Daisy still coming to your sleepover?" said Chloe.

My heart started thumping.

But Emily was quick. "Course she is. We're all coming. Hey, I can't wait till it's *my* sleepover party. If my mum lets me have one."

"*My* mum will let me. She lets me do *anything*. I'm going to have the best sleepover party ever, you'll see," said Chloe.

I was pretty sure I wasn't going to be invited to Chloe's sleepover party. I didn't care. But I did desperately want to go to Amy's.

"Of course you can still come, Daisy," Amy whispered in my ear.

I gave Amy a quick hug. I decided I liked Amy almost as much as Emily.

I went shopping with Mum to buy Amy a birthday present. I thought I might buy her a grown-up fountain pen as she liked writing. I wanted to spend a long time choosing, but Lily was with us too, of course, and she was having a bad day, crying a lot.

People started staring at us and it made Lily more upset. She cried and cried very loudly.

"*Do* hurry up and choose Amy's present!" said Mum.

I couldn't decide which colour fountain pen Amy would like best. Bright red? Lime green? Sunny yellow? Sky blue? Amy liked wearing all different bright colours. I didn't know which was her favourite.

"Daisy! We'll have to go," Mum said.

Lily was bright red in the face herself – and screaming.

I suddenly saw a plastic case of special metallic roller pens all different colours: pink and orange and emerald and purple and turquoise, even gold and silver. I thought how great it would look writing with all these different colours.

"Can I get these for Amy, Mum? Please?"

They were more expensive than the fountain pens but Mum was so keen to get us out of Smith's that she didn't argue.

I hoped Amy would like her special coloured pens. *I'd* have liked a great big set like that. I'd had a lovely purple metallic pen but Lily had got hold of it and spoilt the tip so that it could only write in splotches.

I would have loved to try Amy's pens (just to make sure they worked all right) but as soon as we got home and Mum got Lily changed and fed and calmed down she wrapped Amy's pen set in a piece of pink tissue paper and tied it with my old crimson hair ribbon.

Amy's present looked beautiful. I wished *I* looked beautiful on Saturday afternoon when I was ready to go to the party. Emily had promised me she wouldn't be wearing a proper party dress, just her favourite trousers and T-shirt, so I hadn't

worn my dress either. I had serious doubts about
my dress anyway. It had embroidered teddy bears
all across the chest. I'd liked them at first but now
I felt sure Chloe would say I looked babyish. I
had teddies on my pyjamas too, but I hoped that
wouldn't matter. They were very old pyjamas
 and getting a bit small but they were
my favourites. I also had my *own*
teddy. He's very little and a deep
shade of navy blue. I call him
Midnight. I can't get to sleep
without him, but he's so small I
hoped to hide him in my hand so Chloe couldn't
tease me.

Dad drove me over to Amy's house. I was
very, very, very glad I didn't have to walk there
with Mum and Lily.

"You have a lovely time, Daisy," said Dad,
when we got there.

I didn't say anything.

I hoped and hoped and hoped I *would* have a
lovely time.

* Four *

I was very glad I hadn't worn my teddy dress.
Everyone was wearing tops and trousers. Emily
said she specially liked my top with the silver starry
pattern. I twinkled just like stars.

Amy liked her metallic pens a lot.
"Wow! I *love* these pens. Now I've
got one of every single colour. Let's
try them out, eh?"

"We don't want to do writing at
a party," said Chloe. "Let's play
some music and dance."

So we all trooped into Amy's
living room. It had big red velvet sofas and fluffy
white rugs and lots and lots of china ornaments.
We can't have velvet and furry things at home
because Lily makes too much mess, and she waves
her arms about too much for any china ornaments
to be safe. *We* waved our arms around wildly while
we were dancing but Amy's mum didn't fuss at all,
and she let us have the music up ever so loud.

Amy's two big sisters showed us how to do this brilliant dance. Bella kept turning the wrong way and mixing up her left and right but Alison and Abigail were very patient. I got a *bit* mixed up myself at first but I caught on quite quickly. Quicker than Chloe, actually. Amy knew the dance already so she was very good at it – but not as good as Emily. Emily is magic at dancing.

We did this special dance over and over until we all knew it backwards (though Bella still *faced* backwards if you didn't watch her). Then we performed it like a real girl group to Amy's mum and her dad and her nan and they all clapped and clapped and said we were great.

Then we had our tea and there was the chocolate cake Amy had promised. It was chocolate sponge inside with three layers of chocolate cream and there were even little chocolate drops all round

the frosted chocolate icing on the top of the cake. I had a big slice and it tasted wonderful at first but I couldn't actually finish it. Bella finished it for me. She had her own slice *and* a second helping. Bella is astonishing.

22

When we were all full – even Bella – we watched cartoons on television for a bit, and then we went upstairs with Alison and Abigail and they let us dress up in their special glittery clubbing clothes and stagger round in their high heels. We looked *wonderful*. Almost grown up!

Amy is so lucky having big sisters like Alison and Abigail. Abigail is only three years older than Lily. I imagined what it would be like if Lily's brain hadn't been damaged and she could dress me up in cool clothes and teach me dances.

I felt a little bit sad but then we watched some more funny shows on television – Amy can get ever so many different channels – and I cheered up. I felt especially pleased that when we all sat together on the beautiful red velvet sofa I was in the middle, with Amy one side and Emily the other.

I didn't get so lucky when we all went up to Amy's bedroom to sort out who was sleeping where. Amy has bunk beds so Bella got to go on the top bunk above Amy. Amy's mum had made up a mattress on most of Amy's floor for two more girls.

"That's fine for Emily and me," said Chloe.

"It's a very big mattress," said Emily. "I'm sure there's heaps of room for Daisy too."

"No, it would be much too much of a squash," said Chloe firmly. "Daisy had better have that camp bed thing in the corner."

So I had to make do with the camp bed. It didn't really matter at first because we didn't get *into* bed for hours after we got into our pyjamas. We all played trampolines on the mattress and sang along to tapes on Amy's cassette recorder and painted our nails all different colours with Alison and Abigail's old nail varnishes.

Amy's mum put her head round the door at ten o'clock and said she thought we should start settling down. We didn't settle down for ages and ages. After we'd all gone to the bathroom together and cleaned our teeth (and squirted each other with Amy's dad's shaving foam) Bella said she felt peckish. Amy ran down to the kitchen and came back with a big bag of crisps and the remains of the birthday cake.

We nibbled crisps and ate baby slices of cake as if we were sitting up properly at the tea table, but then we started messing around, scraping icing off the top of the cake with our fingers and seeing how many crisps we could put in our mouths all at once. Bella made herself a chocolate cake crisp sandwich. She said it tasted totally delicious. She wanted us all to try a bite but I decided not to. Emily had a big bite to please Bella –  and then went very, very quiet.

"What's up with you, Emily?" said Chloe. "You're not sleepy already, are you?"

 "No. I just feel a bit sick," said Emily in a tiny voice. 'Yuck! I'm not sure I want to share the mattress with you now. You're not to be sick on me," said Chloe.

"I won't actually *be* sick," said Emily, but she didn't sound too sure.

Amy's mum said we really had to get into

bed now. She looked a little fussed about the crisp crumbs and chocolate smears but she couldn't get really cross on Amy's birthday. She made us all go and clean our teeth again and do a last wee, and then we all got into our different beds and she said good night and switched off the light.

We didn't go to sleep of course. Amy and Bella and Chloe and I talked and talked. Emily didn't say anything.

"Are you asleep, Emily?" I asked.

"No," said Emily.

"You're not still feeling sick, are you?" said Chloe.

"No," said Emily – but after a minute she got out of bed and ran to the bathroom.

"Yuck yuck yuck! She *is* going to be sick," said Chloe.

"Maybe I should call my mum," said Amy.

"I'll go and see if she's all right," I said.

I went to help Emily. When she'd finished being sick I mopped her up and gave her a drink of water and put my arm round her. She was shivering.

"You're so kind, Daisy," she whispered, hugging me back. "I wish you were my best friend."

"I wish I was too."

We both sighed. Then we went back to Amy's room and Emily got into bed with Chloe.

I very quietly fished in my bag and found Midnight. He came underneath the covers with me and we cuddled up in the lonely little camp bed.

Five

It was Bella's birthday next. "I'm going to have a sleepover party too," she said.

"Who's coming?" said Chloe.

I worried.

"We're *all* coming, silly!" said Bella. "It's going to be great. I'm going to have a h-u-g-e cake."

"Is it going to be a chocolate cake?" Emily asked weakly.

"No, it's not. It's going to be a big *blue* cake, and you don't get blue chocolate."

"I didn't think you got blue *cakes*," said Chloe.

"Ah! This is a special one, because my party's going to be extra specially-special," said Bella. "We're all going swimming. My birthday cake's going to have blue icing because it's in the shape of a swimming pool."

We all agreed this *was* specially-special. Even Chloe seemed impressed. "I'm brilliant at swimming. Great idea! Though wait till you hear what I'm doing for *my* sleepover party," she said.

"What?"

"*Aha!*" she said.

"I still don't know if I can *have* a sleepover party," said Emily. "I keep asking my mum and she says there's no point anyone coming to my house because you can't get any sleep as my baby brother cries all night. I *hope* she's just joking. Though she doesn't make many jokes now. She's too tired."

"Never mind, Emily. We don't all have to have sleepover parties," I said quickly. "I'm not sure *my* mum will let me."

"Why? You haven't got a baby brother too, have you?" said Chloe, frowning at me.

"No. I've got a sister, but . . ."

"But what?"

I shrugged, my heart thumping. "Oh. You know," I said – though of course they *didn't* know.

I started madly hoping that Lily might start to get a lot better so that it wouldn't be so bad. Mum said Lily was improving in leaps and bounds now she was at her new special school. Lily couldn't *really* leap or bound. She couldn't walk. She couldn't even crawl.

"But she's on the way to becoming more mobile," said Mum. "She loves her swimming, don't you, Lily? You bob along like a little duck."

Lily's special school had its own small swimming pool. Lily couldn't *really* swim. They just held her in the water while she splashed a bit.

"*I* can swim ever so fast now, Mum," I said. "Hey, did I tell you, Bella's having a special swimming party?"

"You told me lots of times, Daisy," said Mum.

"I do sometimes have to put my foot on the bottom though," I said. "I think Bella and Amy and Emily and Chloe might be able to swim a bit better than me. Especially Chloe."

"Shall I take you swimming on Sunday morning?" said Dad. "Then you can have a little practice swim."

"That's a lovely idea," said Mum. She looked at Lily. I worried that *they* might want to come too.

"Yes, let's, Dad," I said quickly. "Just you and me."

Lily couldn't understand but I felt a bit mean even so. I got into her bed at night and snuggled up to her.

"Do you really like swimming, Lily?" I asked.

Lily went, "Ur ur ur," as if she really did.

"Well, when I get a bit bigger *I'll* take you swimming," I said.

Lily went, "Ur ur ur ur ur," as if she'd like that very much.

I went swimming with Dad on Sunday and we had a great time. Dad showed me how to kick out with my legs like a little frog and I swam ever such a long way without putting my foot down once. Then we played jumping up and down and then Dad pretended he was a dolphin and I rode on his back.

I found a special birthday present for Bella in the swimming pool shop too. Some super-cool turquoise goggles so that she could see under water. I didn't need goggles myself because I didn't actually like going under water.

I was still a bit worried about swimming even after my special practice with Dad – but it was *fine* on Bella's birthday. Emily wasn't very good at swimming either, so most of the time we paddled by the fountains and the plastic palms and played we were shipwrecked on a desert island. Chloe was too busy showing off how far and how fast she could swim to bother about us. Amy was quite good at swimming too, but Bella was the best. She really was brilliant. Bella's dad called her his little water-baby. Bella wasn't exactly *little* but she was certainly a star at swimming. She especially loved swimming underwater. So my turquoise-goggles birthday present was a big success!

When Bella's dad drove us all back to Bella's house we found Bella's mum had her birthday tea all ready for us. It was a HUGE tea. There were six different kinds of sandwiches: egg mayonnaise; chicken; prawn; banana and cream cheese; bacon, lettuce and tomato; and peanut butter and grape jelly. There were six different kinds of cake too:

alphabet fairy cakes; chocolate crispies; chocolate fudge cake; blackcurrant cheesecake; carrot cake; and the special ginormous swimming-pool birth-day cake. It had five little marzipan girls in swimming costumes standing in the middle. It was the most special birthday cake in the world. If I'd been Bella I wouldn't have wanted to eat it, I'd have wanted to keep it for ever.

Bella and I are very different. She cut it all up with a special cake knife and ate two huge slices straight off, *and* all the little marzipan girls.

"Wait till you see *my* birthday cake," said Chloe.

"What's it going to be like?" said Emily.

"*Aha!*" said Chloe.

I was *sick* of Chloe. I was starting to worry about the sleepover part of this party. I was sure I'd be the one left out again. But guess what, guess what, guess what! Bella's mum and dad moved into the spare room. Bella and Amy and Chloe and Emily and I got to sleep in their great big double bed, all of us in together!

It was the greatest fun ever. I was on the outside but I had Emily next to me. I secretly tucked Midnight in the other side, under the covers. We all got the most terrible giggles so that the whole bed wobbled. Bella had a big box of birthday chocolates and kept passing them round. Emily didn't have any. I had two. Amy had three. Chloe had five. Bella had *thirteen*!

We didn't settle down to sleep for ages – and then we got the giggles again because whenever one of us turned over we all had to. Midnight turned too and Emily felt his furry paws. She gave him a special cuddle.

"He's so sweet," she whispered in my ear. "I've got a little teddy called Buttercup. Well, he was a present for my baby brother but *he* just chews his fur so Buttercup's mine now. You'll see him when you come to my house for *my* sleepover party. *If* my mum lets me have one."

* Six *

Emily's mum *did* let her have a sleepover party.

"You're all invited, of course," she said.
"There's too much baby junk in our dining room
to have a proper party tea so mum says we can
all go out for a picnic. I hope that's OK?" Emily
looked a little anxious.

"It's more than OK. It's a simply great idea. I
love picnics," I said. We didn't go on many
picnics ourselves because Lily got upset anywhere
strange and could only eat properly in her special
chair with straps.

"I like picnics too," said Amy.

"Me too. Yum yum. I especially love picnic
food," said Bella.

We all looked a little anxiously at Chloe.

"A picnic is a good idea," said Chloe.
"Though wait till you find out my idea for *my*
sleepover party."

"Do tell us, Chloe," Emily begged.

But Chloe just went, "Aha." I was starting to

think she was just doing it to annoy. Maybe she
didn't have any ideas at all, good or bad.

Chloe saw me staring at her.

"What about *your* sleepover party, Daisy?" she
said.

"What about it?" I said weakly.

"Well, have you got it all sorted out yet?"

"Oh . . . yes. Well. Sort of," I said. "I don't
know a hundred per cent I can *have* my own
sleepover party."

"Don't you worry about it, Daisy," said Emily.
"I had to beg and beg and beg before my mum
said yes."

"But it won't be fair if Daisy doesn't have a
sleepover party. She's been to Amy's and Bella's.
She's coming to Emily's. And she might
be coming to mine. *If* I invite her. So she's *got* to
have one herself. Otherwise she can't be in our

37

Alphabet Girls club and go round with us," said Chloe.

"That's not fair," I said. "It was me that *invented* the Alphabet Club."

"Well, it's a stupid club anyway. We don't really *do* anything," said Chloe.

I was furious. I'd been absolutely brimming over with ideas for things we could do. I'd studied the special alphabet signing language for deaf people (there were all these hand diagrams in my dad's old diary) and I'd tried to teach them to the others so we could have our own secret alphabet language. But Chloe got bored after two minutes and wouldn't try. She wouldn't let the others learn either. I'd suggested we write letters to each other and every time a word contained *our* letter we'd write it in a special colour. Guess what. Chloe said this was too fiddly, and pointless anyway. So *then* I suggested we have a

 competition where we all had shoe boxes and we had to collect in it as many things as possible beginning with our own letter. The one who got the most would get a prize. I even spent my own pocket money on the prize, a special shiny

 notebook with ABCs all over the cover.

Amy and Bella and Emily thought this the best idea ever. Chloe said it *might* be fun. I was pretty proud of this idea myself. I really hoped *I* might get the notebook. I collected Dad's diary and a tiny doll and a drawing pin and a little china dog and dental floss and a Disprin and a dandelion and a mini-doughnut and a plastic dinosaur and a sparkly glass

ring like a diamond. So things were looking good. But Chloe spoilt it all. She filled her shoebox to the brim with chocolate buttons. She must have bought bags and bags of them.

"There are hundreds and hundreds of chocolates!" she said. "So I've won. Give us the notebook then."

"But they are meant to be all *different* things," I said.

"You didn't say so," said Chloe.

"I thought it was obvious."

"It's obvious *you're* just a bad loser," said Chloe. "I want my notebook!"

So I had to give it to her, even though Emily and Amy agreed it wasn't really fair. Bella was too busy helping herself to Chloe's chocolates to comment.

I couldn't stick Chloe. I decided that I didn't *want* to go to her sleepover party. But I very, very badly wanted to go to Emily's. I tried so hard to think of a good birthday present for her. Mum took me shopping on Saturday morning and I spent ages and ages and ages looking at pens and crayons and books but nothing seemed *special* enough for Emily.

Lily was in a good mood at first and slumped to one side, daydreaming, but after an hour she started fussing. Loudly.

"Shut *up*, Lily," I hissed. "Why do you *always* have to spoil things?"

"Hey, hey!" said Mum. "It's not Lily's fault. And she's been really really sweet today. *You're* the one who's grumpy."

"Well, I can't *choose*," I said, nearly in tears. "And Emily's party is this afternoon. I can't be the only one not giving her a present."

"All these birthday presents!" said Mum. "It's

getting a bit much. Still, I suppose it's *your* birthday soon. Are you still keen on this sleepover idea, Daisy?"

"Yes. No. I don't know," I said.

I didn't want to think about my birthday. I wanted to think about Emily's. I was so looking forward to going to her house – and she had said she'd show me her little teddy, Buttercup.

"I've had an idea!" I said.

We went down to the toy department. I searched along a whole shelf of teddy bears. There were great big growly ones, tiny baby ones, plump teddies in silk waistcoats, soft teddies with velvet paws, smiley teddies and sad teddies and silly teddies with goofy faces. And right at the very end of the row was a little girl teddy. She had pink fur and a little blue pinafore frock embroidered with a tiny white flower.

"She's *perfect* for Emily's birthday present!" I said.

* Seven *

Emily loved her bear. She gave me a big hug.

"A bear hug!" she said. "Oh Daisy, she's so sweet. And look, she's got a daisy on her pinafore. I'll *call* her Daisy."

"I think teddies are stupid," said Chloe. "They're for *babies*."

Chloe gave Emily a special CD album of girl singers. She left the price on to show it was very expensive. Emily gave her a hug too. Emily gave everyone a hug. She was so happy she got very pink in the face. She matched Daisy Bear's fur.

Chloe suggested Emily play her new CD so we could all dance but Emily's mum said she'd sooner we didn't play music just at the moment as Emily's little brother Ben was having a nap, and there wasn't really space for us to dance, so perhaps we could all go out in the garden for half an hour while she got the picnic ready.

So we went into the garden with Emily's dad

and played football. Emily got to pick her team first as it was her birthday. She picked Chloe and me. Emily's dad went on Amy and Bella's team but guess what – we still beat them! Emily is very good at football and Chloe is very good at barging into people to stop them getting the ball and, although it sounds like showing off, I happen to be very good at football too.

"We are the champions!" Emily and Chloe and I sang, and we jumped up and down and hugged each other every time we scored a goal. It felt very strange hugging Chloe. Maybe we were proper friends now.

Maybe not. When we were setting off for the picnic Emily suggested I fetch Midnight while she got her Buttercup and brand-new Daisy.

"Yuck! What do you want *them* for?" said Chloe.

"It's a *picnic*, Chloe!" said Emily.

"A teddy bear's picnic!" I said.

We both started singing that funny old teddy bear's picnic song. Amy joined in. Bella joined in.

We sang it in the car. Emily's mum and dad joined in. Emily's baby brother Ben *tried* to join in. Chloe didn't even try. She sat scowling and

sighing and muttering that we were all dead
babyish. When we got out the car at the park
Chloe suddenly gave me a push so that I fell on
my knees and got my new trousers all dirty. It
hurt too. I tried very hard indeed not to cry.

"Did you push Daisy, Chloe?" said Emily's
mum.

"No, of course not. I was just helping her out
the car. It was an accident," said Chloe.

It was accidentally on *purpose*. I hid my face in
Midnight's fur.

"Oh look at little diddums with her teddy-
weddy," Chloe muttered.

I wished Midnight was a real bear and could bite her.

We had another game of football but my knees were bleeding and sticking to my trousers so it was too sore to run. I couldn't be on a team. I had to sit on a rug beside Emily's mum and her little brother Ben.

Still, that wasn't *so* bad. Ben got a bit grizzly so Emily's mum let me give him his bottle. I am very used to helping people drink. I know exactly the right angle.

"You're just like a little mum, Daisy," said Emily's mum. "Have you got a little brother at home?"

"No, I've just got . . . my sister," I said, sitting Ben up and burping him.

"Is she still a baby?" said Emily's mum.

"Not really," I said, vaguely.

"Well, anyway, I'm very glad you and Emily have made friends. You must come round and play whenever you want. You'd be very welcome."

I was so happy I gave Baby Ben a big kiss on his button nose. Emily's mum was frowning over at Chloe who was stamping her foot and complaining because Amy and Bella had managed to score a goal. She didn't look as if Chloe was very welcome at all!

I gave a great grin. Emily smiled back at me and came running over. "How are your poor knees, Daisy?" she said.

"*Emily!* Come back. You're the *goalie!*" Chloe screeched.

"I'm not playing any more. It's not really fair playing football when Daisy can't join in," said Emily.

"Anyway, now that we've got Ben fed I think it's time for our picnic," said Emily's mum quickly, before Chloe could make any further fuss.

The picnic was *delicious*: chicken drumsticks and tiny tomatoes and crusty French bread and crisps and apples and cherry flapjacks and a yellow birthday cake in the shape of a teddy bear! Emily insisted Daisy Bear and Buttercup and Midnight all had tiny slices too.

"I wish I'd brought *my* teddy along," said Bella. "This is yummy cake, Emily. Though I think chocolate's still my favourite. You haven't got anything chocolatey at all."

"I've gone off chocolate," said Emily firmly.

She seemed to have gone off Chloe too! When we got changed into our pyjamas back at Emily's house it hurt pulling my trousers off and my knees bled a bit. Emily looked shocked.

"Your poor knees, Daisy," she said. She looked hard at Chloe. "Look at the state of Daisy's knees, Chloe," she said sternly.

Chloe shrugged. "It was an accident, I *said*."

"Poor Daisy," said Bella.

"Yes, you're being ever so brave, Daisy," said Amy.

Emily put her arm round me while Emily's mum gave my knees a wash and put stingy stuff on them and bandaged them carefully.

"I don't see why everyone's making such a fuss about Daisy's boring old knees," Chloe muttered. "They're just scratched, that's all."

"Do shut up, Chloe," said Emily.

Then you'll never guess what. Emily said I could share *her* bed for the sleepover. Amy and Bella shared the other bed. And Chloe had to have the spare mattress all by herself.

Eight

I was certain Chloe wasn't going to invite me to her sleepover party. Especially now that Emily was very nearly my best friend too.

Chloe had special invitations. They were all different colours. Emily had a red envelope, Bella a blue, Amy an orange. Surprise, surprise. I didn't have an invitation.

"What about Daisy?" said Emily.

"Who?" said Chloe, as if she'd never even heard of me.

"You are funny, Chloe! *Daisy*," said Emily, putting her arm round me.

"You didn't forget Daisy, did you?" said Amy.

"I didn't forget her," said Chloe. "But my mum says I can only have three people at my sleepover party. So that's Emily and Amy and Bella. Right?"

"That's all *wrong*," said Emily. She was going very pink in the face.

"It's not fair on Daisy," said Amy.

"Poor Daisy," said Bella, giving me a squeeze.

"Yes, poor Daisy," said Chloe, as if she was really sorry. As if!

"Daisy's got to come too, Chloe!" said Emily, getting even pinker.

"Look, it's not *my* fault. It's my *mum*."

"Your mum lets you do anything you want, you know she does. You're just not being fair," said Emily.

"It *is* fair, because I've been to your sleepover party, Emily, and I've been to Amy's and I've been to Bella's. I haven't been to Daisy's. She doesn't even know for definite if she's going to *have* a sleepover party," said Chloe.

"You're just being *mean*, Chloe," said Emily.

"Don't you start getting all stroppy with me, Emily, or you won't be coming to my sleepover party either, even if you are my best friend," said Chloe.

"It's OK, Emily," I whispered.

"It's *not* OK," said Emily. "I don't want to come to your sleepover party if Daisy can't come too."

50

She stared very fiercely at Amy and Bella. "You don't want to either, do you?" she said.

Amy and Bella looked uncertain. But then Bella nodded and said, "That's right, Emily." And Amy nodded too.

Chloe glared at Amy and Bella. She looked as if she might hit Emily. She seemed all set to *murder* me.

"See if I care then," she said, and she flounced off.

"Oh dear," said Amy.

"She said she was going to have a gigantic chocolate cake at her party," said Bella, sighing.

"She's really going to have it in for me now," said Emily. "You know what she can be like. I've tried and tried to stop being friends with Chloe – but it's better to have her as your friend than your deadly enemy."

"It's all my fault!" I said, feeling truly dreadful.

Emily and Bella and Amy were very comforting but I still felt bad. I didn't tell Mum when I got home from school. I didn't tell Dad when he got home from work.

I waited until it was bedtime and then I crept into Lily's bed and cuddled up with her and told her all about it.

Lily went, "Ur ur ur ur ur."

I decided that was Lily-language for, "That Chloe is a mean hateful pig."

"I'm scared she'll be really, really horrible now," I whispered. "I'm *used* to her being mean to me. But it'll be so awful if she's mean to Emily too."

Lily went, "Ur ur ur ur ur," as if she were saying, "Don't you worry about it, Daisy."

I did worry. Lots and lots. I didn't sleep much that night. But guess what. Chloe dropped a pink envelope on my desk in the morning.

"I got my mum to change her mind," she said. "You're coming to my sleepover party now, Daisy. And you, Emily. And Bella and Amy."

"Oh *great*, Chloe!" said Emily, and she gave her a big hug. "Isn't that wonderful, Daisy?"

I wasn't sure.

I was even less sure when Chloe whispered in

my ear, "I don't *really* want you to come, Daisy Diddums."

I didn't want to get Chloe a birthday present. Especially a birthday present she'd really, really like. But when Dad and I went down the video shop on Friday night they were having a special sale and there was this video called "The Spooky Sleepover" and I knew it would be just perfect for Chloe.

Mum was a bit cross with Dad for buying it.

"It's much too scary for a little girl," she said.

"It sounds like this Chloe is much scarier than any soppy video," said Dad.

He took me to the party on Saturday because he said he couldn't wait to meet Chloe. He looked a bit taken aback when he saw her. Chloe is little and cute and she's got big blue eyes and these blonde curls. It's pretty sickening actually.

Chloe gave me this great big false smile when my dad was still there.

"Ooh, what a super-sounding video! I hope it's not too frightening. Thank you ever so much, Daisy," said Chloe.

But the second Dad was gone Chloe stuck her tongue out at me and dropped the video on the floor.

"I saw this ages ago and it sucks. It isn't spooky at all. Trust you to pick a *baby* film, Daisy Diddums."

Nine

"Come on, Diddums," said Chloe. "We're all in the kitchen. I suppose you'd better come too."

Chloe's kitchen was amazingly big and posh and shiny with all sorts of cupboards and ovens and machines. Chloe's mum was as shiny as her kitchen. She wore a white glittery top and white satin trousers, with a little pink-and-white frilly apron over the top. She looked more like Chloe's sister than her mum.

Emily and Amy and Bella were all standing at a crowded table with big aprons pinned around them and their sleeves rolled up.

"Hi, Daisy!" said Emily. "We're all making our own pizzas – it's such fun."

"We can choose any topping we like," said Amy, arranging pepperoni in a noughts and crosses shape on her pizza.

"I'm making a Bellaroni special," Bella giggled, squirting chocolate sauce everywhere.

"See, I *said* I was going to have a brilliant

sleepover party," said Chloe. "The best in the whole world."

"For the best little girl in the whole world," said Chloe's dad, popping his head round the door.

Chloe's mum was very young, but Chloe's dad was quite old, with a bald head and a big fat tummy. He made a pizza too – with *all* the toppings.

"Wow!" said Bella, seriously impressed.

"What are you going to put on your pizza, Daisy?" asked Emily.

I thought hard.

"I'm going to make mine a face," I said.

I sprinkled lots of grated cheese on the top half for hair. Then I did olives for eyes and a slice of yellow pepper for a nose and a curvy red pepper slice for a smiley mouth. I placed a  tomato each side for rosy cheeks and I used pineapple chunks for gold earrings and a choker necklace.

"Oh Daisy, you are *clever*," said Emily.

"It looks so good you won't want to eat it," said Bella.

"How about a couple of anchovies for eyebrows?" said Amy.

"No! They'd look good but I *hate* anchovies," I said. I think they look like grey slimy worms. They always give me the shudders.

Chloe didn't say anything. But when we all followed Chloe's dad into their dining room Chloe hung back to help her mum put the pizzas into the giant oven.

Chloe's dad pretended to be a barman and fixed us all a fruit-juice cocktail. They didn't just have little paper umbrellas like at Amy's. They had tiny plastic Mickey Mouse stirrers and cherries on sticks and ice-cubes in the shape of stars.

We all clinked glasses and when Chloe came into the dining room we sang *Happy Birthday*. Chloe's dad conducted us and got all watery-eyed at the end. Then he seated us at the dining table. We each had a little present on our side plate. It was a little letter charm on a silvery bracelet. A B C D and E. Chloe's C was gold and her bracelet was a proper gold link one with little golden hearts.

"Real gold for our birthday girl," said her dad.

"And look, I've got real gold heart earrings to match," said Chloe, looping her curls behind her ears. "I had them pierced as an extra birthday present."

We all stared at her ears enviously. My mum says I'm going to have to wait right up until I'm *sixteen* before I'm allowed to have my ears pierced.

Chloe's mum came in with the first two pizzas. She'd taken her apron off. Her T-shirt top was so tiny it showed her bare tummy and she'd had her belly button pierced! It looked truly cool. I hadn't realized mums could have curvy waists and flat tummies. My mum hasn't.

Chloe's mum served Chloe and Emily with their pizzas. Then she fetched Amy's and Bella's.

"Are you sure you meant to use *chocolate* sauce, Bella?" said Chloe's mum, putting Bella's very brown pizza in front of her.

"Oh yes, yummy! Chocolate's my favourite

58

thing in all the world," said Bella happily.

"Well, I'll fetch you some chocolate drops to put on top, if you like," said Chloe's mum, laughing.

She was joking but Bella said, "Yes, please!"

Chloe's mum went to get Bella some chocolate drops – and she brought my pizza too.

"You must love anchovies even more than Bella loves chocolate, Daisy," said Chloe's mum.

I stared at her. I stared at my pizza. There was still a face with cheesy hair and olive eyes and a pepper mouth. But all the plain skin gaps in between were filled in with grey slimy anchovies. Hundreds of them!

"It looks very effective, my love, but I'm really not sure you should eat so many anchovies. You'll make yourself sick," said Chloe's mum.

"I – I don't like anchovies," I whispered.

"Then why on earth put them on your pizza?" said Chloe, snorting with laughter.

I hadn't put them on my pizza.

I knew who *had*.

It must have been Chloe herself. But I couldn't say anything at her own party. And Chloe's mum and dad wouldn't have believed me anyway. They thought Chloe was the best little girl in the world. I knew she was the *worst*.

I tried to eat the cheesy hair on my pizza but the anchovies had even got under there. It was as if they were still alive and had wriggled everywhere. I couldn't swallow a mouthful.

"That was a bit of a waste, Daisy," said Chloe's mum. "Still, never mind. I'm sure you can fill up on Chloe's birthday cake."

 Chloe had the biggest cake in the whole world. It was in three tiers, just like a wedding cake. The bottom layer was fruitcake with extra cherries and bright yellow marzipan under the white icing. The middle layer was chocolate fudge cake with lots of chocolate buttercream. The top layer was vanilla sponge with strawberry jam and fresh cream. It had HAPPY BIRTHDAY, CHLOE, SWEETHEART in silver iced writing with silver hearts studded all around the edge.

"We'll make sure *your* slice has a special anchovy filling, Daisy," Chloe whispered.

I think she might have been joking this time. But I couldn't take any chances. I didn't eat a bite of this most beautiful birthday cake. I sat and watched the others eating it. (Bella had a big slice from each layer.)

I felt my lips go trembly and my eyes starting pricking but I was absolutely determined not to cry in front of Chloe.

I didn't cry later on when we all went up to Chloe's bedroom and I saw I'd been put in a sleeping bag all by myself over by the door.

I didn't cry when we all watched a scary horror movie on Chloe's television about an evil child with a teddy bear possessed by the devil. He smothered all these little kids but he ended up being horribly ripped to bits. I was very glad Midnight was still zipped up in my overnight bag or *he* might have cried.

I didn't cry when we all got ready for bed and it was my turn in the loo and the lock didn't work properly and Chloe suddenly opened the door on me and everyone laughed.

I didn't cry when we all got into bed (I got into bag) and we watched a much, much, much scarier horror movie about a witchy white ghost who crept up on these girls in a college dormitory and murdered them one by one.

"This is *too* scary, Chloe," Emily said.

"It's like it's *real*," said Amy, sucking her thumb.

"Can't we watch some other movie?" said Bella. "I'm not going to be able to sleep for worrying about the witchy white ghost."

"It's OK," said Chloe. "If the witchy white ghost comes creeping up on us she'll get Daisy first as she's the one nearest the door! And anyway you don't *sleep* at a sleepover party."

I certainly didn't sleep. I stayed awake all night long, hunched into a ball in my sleeping bag, clutching Midnight tight. But then he nearly turned into Devil Bear and wanted to smother me. I had to grip him in my knees. They were right up under my chin because there might be anchovies wriggling round the bottom of the sleeping bag. And all the time the witchy white ghost wailed just outside the bedroom door, waiting to come and get me . . .

* Ten *

"Not long now till your birthday, Daisy," said Mum.

I didn't say anything.

Lily went, "Ur ur ur ur ur." She was lying on the rug and I was tickling her.

"I suppose you want to have a sleepover party too," said Mum.

I didn't say anything.

Lily went, "UR UR UR UR UR!"

"Daisy! I'm talking to you! And stop tickling Lily."

"She likes it. Don't you, Lily?" I said.

"URRR URRR URRR URRR URRR!"

"She'll get over-excited. Stop it, now."

"URRRRRRRRRRR! URRRRRRR-RRR!"

Lily got so over-excited she started wailing and wouldn't stop. She cried until she was sick. Mum had to take her upstairs to change her and calm her down.

Lily's wails were very weak and tired now. At least she always slept for ages after one of her bad crying fits. At last she went quiet.

It was very quiet in the living room too. I looked at Dad. I thought he was cross with me. He switched on the television. Then he switched it off. He patted his knee.

"Want to come and have a cuddle?" he said.

I was surprised but very pleased. I tucked in beside Dad and he put his arm round me and kissed the top of my head. Then he pretended he was a sheep and my hair was grass so he went gobble gobble munch munch.

"I love this game. We haven't played it for ages!" I said.

"I'll try to get home from work early more often," Dad said. "I don't get to see enough of you, Daisy. And poor Mum is always so busy with Lily."

"Yes," I said, sighing. "Sorry I made her get upset," I added in a tiny voice.

"That's OK, pet. You were only playing," said Dad.

"Yes, but I was playing a bit too much," I said.

"Don't let's talk about Lily. Let's talk about you – and this birthday of yours," said Dad.

I didn't say anything.

"What's up?"

"Nothing," I said.

"Nothing!" said Dad. "Maybe I'm going to start tickling *you* unless you tell me what's making you look so worried. Come on, my little glum chum." He tickled me under my chin and I collapsed, squeaking and spluttering.

"Don't! Please don't!"

"Well, tell me what's the matter."

"There's nothing the matter, Dad, honest. It's just . . . I don't really want a sleepover party for my birthday."

"But I thought they were all the rage. Just recently you've been to heaps."

"I know."

"So you really need to invite everyone back."

"But . . . I don't want to."

"Why?"

I fidgeted.

Dad put his head close to mine.

"Is it because of Lily?" he whispered.

"A bit," I whispered back.

"We'll explain about Lily to your friends."

"But they might still be a bit funny about it. Not Emily. She's ever so special. And Bella's lovely too. And Amy. It's just . . . Chloe. Chloe's *horrible*."

"The little curly-haired one?" said Dad.

"Her," I said grimly.

"Oh well, it's easy-peasy," said Dad. "Invite Emily and Bella and Amy to your sleepover birthday party and leave Chloe out."

"*Really?*"

"Of course. It's your birthday. You don't have to invite anyone you don't want," said Dad.

"But Emily and Amy and Bella said it wasn't fair when Chloe tried not to invite me to *her* sleepover."

"Do they all like Chloe?"

"Well . . . I think they're just a bit scared of her."

"Then they'll probably be glad she's not invited," said Dad.

"I'll be ever so, ever so glad!" I said, bouncing up and down on Dad's knee.

"That's it, little Smiley-Face. All settled," said Dad, beaming.

But it wasn't settled.

Mum said I had to invite Chloe too.

"It's only fair. You went to Chloe's party, Daisy, so she has to come to yours."

"But she didn't want me to come, Mum! She tried hard *not* to invite me. She's really mean to me, Mum. She gangs up on me at school and she was extra-awful to me at her party."

"Why didn't you tell me?"

"I *am* telling you!"

"No, at the time, silly."

"You were busy with Lily. You're *always* busy with Lily."

"No, I'm not. Not always. Anyway, I'm afraid I've already invited Chloe. Her mother rang up after her party because she was worried you might be sickening for something. She said you didn't eat anything, poppet."

"Ha! Chloe put anchovies all over my pizza!" I shuddered so hard I nearly fell out of Dad's armchair.

"Oh dear. Well, I told Chloe's mum you'd be having a sleepover party yourself and I automatically invited Chloe."

"Can't we un-invite this foul little girl?" said Dad, giving me a hug.

"Not really. It would look awful."

"*She's* awful."

"She won't be able to be awful to you at our house, not when it's your special party, Daisy."

I was sure Chloe would find a way.

I didn't say any more to Dad. I didn't say any more to Mum. But after they were asleep I crept into bed beside Lily. She'd been asleep for hours and hours but she was awake now. "I hate Chloe," I said.

"Ur ur ur ur ur," said Lily, comfortingly, as if she hated her too.

"She's so mean to me," I said.

"Ur ur ur ur ur," said Lily.

I thought for a little while.

"I'm sometimes mean to you, Lily," I said. "Do you hate me sometimes?"

"Ur ur ur ur ur," said Lily. "Ur ur ur ur *ur*."

I hoped she was saying she didn't hate me at all, she loved me because I was her sister.

"Well, I love you because you're *my* sister, Lily," I said. "And if Chloe is mean to you I'll smack her hard, you just wait and see."

* Eleven *

Mum and Dad sang *Happy Birthday* to me on Saturday morning. Lily sang too, screeching louder and louder: "UR UR UR UR UR!"

"She's getting over-excited again, Mum," I said.

"Never mind," said Mum.

"We're *all* over-excited because it's your birthday, Daisy," said Dad.

I had a special birthday breakfast of croissants and cherry jam and hot chocolate – yummy yummy.

"Do you think we can have more hot chocolate later on for my party?" I said. "I think Bella would like it a lot."

"Yes, of course," said Mum.

"But Emily doesn't like chocolate any more," I worried.

"We'll find something else for Emily."

"Something special – because Emily's my almost best friend," I said.

"What shall we serve Chloe?" said Dad, winking. "A mug of greasy lukewarm washing-up water?"

I fell about laughing. Mum frowned, but she couldn't stop herself giggling too.

After breakfast Mum got Lily ready and then Dad took her for a long walk in her wheelchair while Mum and I cleared up and then made my birthday cake together. Mum let me stir the mixture and spoon it out into the cake tin. She let me scrape the mixing bowl with the spoon (and then my finger and *then* my tongue!). We made white chocolate crunch biscuits while the cake was cooling and *then* we did the decorating.

Mum got a very sharp knife and started cutting the cake.

"Mum! *I* cut the cake. It's my birthday. What

are you doing? The cake isn't even finished yet."

"I know. I *am* finishing it. I'm turning it into a special cake," said Mum. "Watch."

I watched. Mum cut delicate little wedges out of the cake every so often. She was turning the cake into a particular shape. Then I suddenly realized.

"It's a *daisy*! Oh Mum, how brilliant!"

Mum defined each petal perfectly. Then we mixed up some bright white icing and carefully covered it all over.

"It looks lovely!" I said, putting a little smear of icing on one of the cut-off wedges. "Yum! It tastes lovely too."

"It's not quite finished yet," said Mum.

She coloured the left-over icing yellow and spread that in a neat circle in the middle so that

72

the cake looked just like a real daisy. When it was all dry she iced HAPPY BIRTHDAY DAISY in pink on top. It looked *so* beautiful, especially when Mum slid the cake onto our best green plate. All round the edges she put little daisy hairslides. I counted. Twenty four. Enough for everyone to have four – and Emily and I could have six.

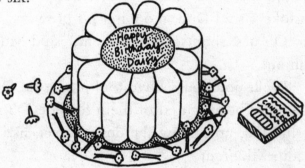

"No, no, four each," said Mum.

"Emily, me, Bella, Amy and Chloe, yuck yuck. Five times four is twenty."

"There are six of you, silly. What about Lily?" said Mum.

"But Lily isn't part of the sleepover party," I said.

"Of course she is! She's your sister."

"Lily can't do her own hair so she doesn't need hairslides."

"You could do her hair for her. And I'm sure she'll love her daisy hairslides," said Mum. "Oh, there's Lily and Dad back now. Did you have a lovely walk, Lily? What's all that silly noise for?"

"UR UR UR UR UR!" Lily wailed.

"I took her round the shopping centre. I thought she'd like those giant teddies. *Big* mistake," said Dad, mopping his brow.

"Oh yes, she's scared of them," said Mum, sighing.

"Well, you could have told me," said Dad.

"Lily's been scared of them for ages," I said. "Oh, Dad, you know she doesn't even like my teddy, Midnight."

"Come on, Lily, let's mop those weepy eyes and wipe that poor nose," said Mum. "And stop that noise, *please*!"

"Ur ur ur ur ur," Lily mumbled, sniffling.

Mum started to carry Lily upstairs.

"Oh dear, she needs changing too. Look, you two had better get started on Daisy's bedroom. Though how all four girls are going to squash in there I just don't know."

"Lots of girls use the living room for sleepovers," I suggested.

74

"There's even less space in our living room," said Dad, "what with Lily's special chair and her rug and all her other stuff. Then he looked at the window. He looked out of the window.

"I know!" said Dad. "Daisy, how about having your sleepover in the garden? We could get the tent out the loft."

"Oh, Dad! Magic!" I said.

We went racing up the stairs past Mum and Lily so that Dad could climb up in the loft. We bought all the camping stuff last year for our summer holiday. We can't usually stay in a hotel because it's so difficult with Lily. It was difficult camping with her too. She cried most of the night. And the next, even though I got in her sleeping bag with her. She didn't like it because it was different. The third night Lily cried and Mum cried too. Dad didn't cry but he said, "This is ridiculous," and we packed up the tent and drove home in the middle of the night.

"I knew that tent would come in useful eventually," Dad said now, and he unpacked it and took it out into the garden.

"It's going to be so cool!" I said.

"Too cool, literally,' said Mum. "It'll be freezing cold in the middle of the night."

"The girls can all wrap up really warmly. They'll have a whale of a time," said Dad.

"But Lily won't be able to join in any of the fun. You know what she's like in that tent," said Mum.

"You don't have to remind me!" said Dad.

I didn't say anything.

I couldn't help feeling very glad indeed that Lily wouldn't be able to join in.

Twelve

I wore my starry T-shirt and my new birthday-present jeans with embroidered daisies up and down the legs. I couldn't wait to have the daisy hairslides in my hair to match.

"You look lovely, Daisy," said Mum.

"Our special birthday girl," said Dad.

"Ur ur ur ur ur," said Lily softly. I wondered if she really knew it was my birthday. I wondered if she ever knew when it was her birthday.

I wondered if Lily wished she could wear tiny T-shirts and embroidered jeans. Lily mostly wore big towelling tops because she dribbled and spilt so much and they stopped her getting too wet. She wore loose jogging trousers because they were easy to whip on and off when she needed changing. Lily's clothes were practical but they weren't *pretty*.

Lily wasn't pretty either. Mum kept her very clean but her face went funny and she always looked lopsided because she couldn't sit up properly. She did have lovely long hair though.

"Wait till after my party, Lily," I said, giving her a hug. "We'll play hairdressers and I'll fix your hair with daisy slides. You'll like them. You'll look dead cool in them."

"Ur ur ur ur ur!" said Lily excitedly.

"Try not to get her too worked up, pet," Mum said gently.

"We don't want her roaring her head off when your party guests come," said Dad.

We all waited. We were all a bit worried. I was sure Chloe was going to say something terrible about Lily. And I wasn't sure that Amy and Bella would be ultra-tactful. And maybe even Emily would act oddly about Lily and then what would I do?

My new birthday jeans suddenly seemed much too tight. I had a horrible squeezy feeling in my tummy. I wished I wasn't having a sleepover party. I wished Mum would take Lily and hide her away for the whole weekend.

Amy arrived first. "Hi, Daisy. Happy birthday!"

She gave me a pink plastic make-up bag with silver nail varnish and a pot of silver face glitter. I was so thrilled I forgot all about Lily for one tiny moment.

"Ur ur ur," said Lily in the background, determined not to be forgotten.

Amy jumped, startled. She looked at Lily in her special chair.

"That's Lily," I said. "She's my sister."

"Hi, Lily," Amy said uncertainly.

"Ur ur," said Lily.

"What's wrong with her?" Amy hissed.

"Something happened to her brain when she was born," I said.

"Oh dear," said Amy. "So can't she walk?"

"No."

"Well . . . she can sort of talk," said Amy.

"Yes, she can. And she can shout too!" I said.

79

I felt a lot, lot, lot better. I *did* like Amy. Maybe second best to Emily instead of Bella.

Bella arrived next.

"Hello, Daisy. Here, happy birthday!"

She gave me a big box of chocolates with a puppy picture on the lid and a purple ribbon which would come in useful for future hairdressing sessions. Bella glanced at Lily and nodded. Then she looked back at the chocolates. Hopefully.

"Are you going to open them now?" said Bella.

"OK. Oh, they look really yummy!" I said.

I handed the box to Bella.

"You should choose first as it's your birthday," Bella said, which was good of her, because she was staring hard at the biggest white chocolate in the middle.

"You have that one as you gave them to me," I said, offering it to her. Bella didn't need persuading. I chose a round chocolate with a rose petal on top. Amy chose a chocolate wrapped in gold paper.

Bella took the box over to Lily.

"Do you want a chocolate?"

"Ur ur ur," said Lily.

"What did you say?" said Bella.

"Lily can't really say stuff," I said, going over to her. "She likes chocolate, but just a weeny bit, so she can't choke." I broke a tiny piece off my rose chocolate and popped it in Lily's open mouth.

"Poor Lily. Fancy choking on chocolate!" said Bella.

I decided I liked Bella and Amy second-best equal to Emily.

Emily arrived next. She had a star T-shirt on exactly the same as mine! "Happy birthday, Daisy," she said. "Hey, we're the star twins. We can go twinkle twinkle!"

She gave me my birthday present. I felt it first. It was quite squashy, with a little round bit. The round bit went grur-grur-grur when I squeezed it.

"Ur ur ur !" said Lily excitedly, as if they spoke the same language.

Emily looked surprised.

"Hello," she said.

"This is Lily," I said. "She's my sister."

"Hi, Lily," said Emily. She paused. "I like your hair. I'm trying to grow mine but it's taking *ages*."

"Ur ur ur," said Lily. She smiled as if she understood.

I smiled too. I knew Emily was the nicest friend in the whole world.

I unwrapped my birthday present. It was a beautiful new pair of pyjamas, white with yellow buttons and a pattern of little yellow teddy bears – and in the pyjama pocket there was a tiny toy teddy.

"He's called Little Growler. Press his tummy!" said Emily. "That was him growling before. Lily liked it."

But Lily hadn't realized grur-grur-grur was Beartalk. Lily hates bears. She's even scared of tiny teddy bears like Little Growler.

She saw him – and she started. "UR UR UR UR UR!" Lily wailed.

"Oh goodness, what's the matter?" said Emily.

"*UR UR UR UR UR!*" Lily screamed.

"What's the matter?" said Amy.

"Has she hurt herself?" said Bella.

"She's just a bit frightened. She'll be all right in a minute," I said. But she wasn't.

Mum had to cart Lily upstairs to calm her down. Lily wouldn't calm down one bit. She roared.

We heard her being sick.

"Oh dear," said Emily. "Will she be all right now?"

"I think she'll need to go to sleep for a while," said Dad.

We listened. Lily's cries were getting weaker.

"Poor Lily, she'll miss all the fun," said Amy.

"She'll miss her tea if she goes to sleep," said Bella.

I crossed my fingers. I hoped Lily would sleep for hours and hours and hours.

Thirteen

Chloe was so late I began to think she wasn't coming. My heart started thumping under my twinkle-star T-shirt. My sleepover party would be just for four. Amy and Bella – and Emily and me! Emily might be *my* best friend. I felt I was flying right up to the real stars.

But then I came down to earth with a bump. There was a knock at the door. Chloe was here.

"Happy birthday, Daisy," she cooed, all smiles in front of her mum. (*My* mum was still upstairs sorting out Lily.)

Chloe had a new T-shirt on too. It had sparkly pink lettering. It said: *The Bestest Little Girl in all the World*. Chloe had pink sparkles on her cheeks and pink lipstick and pink strappy shoes with real heels.

Her present was wrapped up in sparkly pink paper too. I opened it gingerly. I was expecting a parcel of anchovies. But it was a video. It had *101 Dalmations* on the cover. But 101 Doubts rushed round my head like little dogs. I didn't trust Chloe. Not one bit.

We went into the living room to play. Mum had tried to tidy it up but Lily's special bouncy chair was still there.

"What a weird chair!" said Chloe.

"It's my sister's," I said.

"But it's ginormous. She must be a *huge* baby." Chloe blew out her cheeks and waddled like a giant toddler. "Where is she then? Has she crawled off somewhere?" said Chloe, pretending to look under the table.

"She's upstairs with my mum. She's putting her to bed because she got over-excited."

"Oh, poor little baba. You'd better watch out, Daisy Diddums. You might get over-excited and put to bed too," said Chloe. She paused. "Well, what are we going to do, then?"

I hadn't quite sorted it out.

"Let's dance," said Amy.

But I didn't have the right sort of music.

"Yuck, this is all baby stuff – or *ancient*," said Chloe, flipping through our CDs.

"Maybe we can have tea now?" said Bella.

But it was still a bit early for tea, and anyway, Mum was still upstairs with Lily.

"Shall we go out in the garden and play football?" said Emily.

So we went out in the garden, but nearly all the grass was taken up with the tent. Dad was just sorting out the last few tent pegs, hitting them with a wooden mallet.

"Hi, girls!" he said.

"Ooh, a tent!" said Emily.

"I've always wanted to go camping," said Amy.

"Can we have campfire food?" said Bella.

"We can't play football with that stupid tent there. Shame you've got such a *little* garden."

"Ah, it's Daisy's special friend Chloe," said Dad, giving her a funny smile. "Are you having fun, girls?"

"Yes," said Emily politely.

"No," said Chloe.

"We don't know what to do, Dad," I said desperately.

"Ah. I think Mum was going to sort you girls out before tea – but she's still with Lily, is she? Tell you what! Why don't you play party games?"

"Party games? Like what?" I said.

"Like, *boring*," said Chloe.

"No, no, they're good fun," Dad insisted. "Let's all go indoors and play."

When Chloe turned to go Dad mimed hitting her over the head with his wooden mallet. Emily and Amy and Bella and I all fell about laughing.

"What's so funny?" said Chloe crossly.

"Nothing. We're just having fun," I said.

And we *did* have fun. Dad showed us how to play all these weird old-fashioned party games like Squeak Piggy Squeak. When Chloe was the pig she sat on my lap so hard I squeaked for real but I didn't care.

Then we played Stations and I was Clapham Junction and Emily was Vauxhall and we had to keep swapping and once we bumped into each other and got the giggles. Chloe was Waterloo and she bumped into me on purpose and stamped on my toe but I didn't care.

Then we played Murder in the Dark and I got a bit worried Chloe would be the murderer and if she pretended to murder me it might hurt rather a lot. Luckily Bella was the murderer and she just gave me a tiny poke in the tummy and whispered, "Ever so sorry but you're dead now, Daisy." Chloe kept pretending to trip over me all the time I was the Dead Body and each time she tripped she kicked. I tried hard not to care.

Dad saw one time and said, "Hey, Chloe, don't kick Daisy like that!"

Chloe went red as she's not used to being told off.

"I'm sick of playing this silly game. Let's do something else," she said.

So we played Musical Bumps. It was great fun. Even Chloe cheered up and started jumping to the music, even if it *was* ancient. I wondered if it might start Lily off again but Mum came down at last and muttered to Dad that she was fast asleep.

"So I'll fix tea," said Mum.

Everyone loved my beautiful Daisy cake. Mum even cut the sandwiches with a special cutter so they were daisy-shaped too. We drank our lemonade out of green glasses and had little white iced buns and white chocolate clusters and green grape jelly and vanilla ice-cream.

"I love the way it all matches," said Amy.

"It looks almost too lovely to eat," said Emily.

"*Almost*," said Bella, tucking in straight away.

We all tucked in. We ate and ate until we were very nearly full. Then I had to cut my birthday cake ever so carefully. As the knife sliced through the thick icing and soft sponge and gooey jam I made my birthday wish.

"I wish Emily could be my best friend," I whispered to myself.

Then everyone sang *Happy Birthday To You*. When they got to "*Happy* Birthday, dear Daisy," Chloe sang "*Diddums Daisy*" but I didn't care.

The birthday cake was delicious. I hoped Mum might make cakes more often! She washed all the daisy hairslides for us because some had got a bit sticky with icing and then she handed them out.

"There are four left over. Can I have them seeing as I've got the longest curliest hair?" said Chloe.

"No, dear, those slides are for Lily," said Mum.

"Daisy's sister? Babies don't wear hairslides!" said Chloe.

I held my breath. But Bella asked if it would be terribly piggy if she had just one more slice of birthday cake. Dad laughed and offered her the whole plateful.

"I wouldn't do that! She'll eat it all!" said Amy.

"And she doesn't *ever* feel sick," said Emily.

"You're just a greedy-guts, Bella," said Chloe. "You'll grow into a great big whale and never be able to wear decent clothes."

"Whales don't need clothes. They swim around and spout at silly little tadpoles like you," said Bella.

She pretended to spout at Chloe, but she still had a large mouthful of cake. Chloe's *Bestest*

Little Girl in the Whole World T-shirt got sprayed with crumbs. We all fell about laughing. Chloe didn't find it funny at all.

"You disgusting pig, Bella," she said, and she pushed her off her chair.

"Hey, hey, that's enough!" said Mum. "I think it's time you all got down from the table. Daisy, run and find one of your T-shirts, poppet, so Chloe can wear it while I put her own in the washing machine."

Chloe followed me up the stairs. Amy and Bella and Emily came too. I tiptoed past Lily's door.

"Why are you walking like that?" Chloe asked.

"Sh! Lily's asleep," I whispered.

Emily and Amy and Bella all started walking on tiptoe too. Chloe went STOMP STOMP CLACKETY CLUMP in her heeled shoes . . . but thank goodness Lily didn't stir in her room.

91

Everyone squashed into my room.

"Goodness, isn't it weeny?" said Chloe.

"No, it's not," said Bella.

"It's a lovely room," said Amy.

"It's the nicest room I've ever seen," said Emily.

It's not. It *is* weeny. Lily has a proper size bedroom because she's got so much stuff and Mum sometimes sleeps on a campbed beside her if she's having a bad spell. I have to make do with the tiny bedroom – but Dad's put up special shelves on my

wall with a roof on top, like a big open dolls' house so all my books and paints and stuff have different "rooms". Mum's made me a duvet cover and curtains patterned with dolls' houses and on my window sill I have my *real* dolls' house. A very tiny family of teddy bears live inside. Midnight is too big but he sometimes likes to squeeze up really small and visit them.

"Dolls' houses are for babies!" said Chloe.

"No, they're not. My gran collects dolls' houses and she's an old lady," said Emily. "I'm not really allowed to play with her dolls' houses though."

"You can play with mine," I said.

"We're not playing baby doll games," said Chloe. "Come on then, Daisy, show me all your T-shirts."

I showed her my blue T-shirt with the dolphin and my pink T-shirt with little flowers and my black T-shirt with the silver mermaid (only the silver comes off so she hasn't got a tail any more).

"Is this all you've *got*?" said Chloe.

She chose the dolphin T-shirt though she sneered at it and said it was stupid. She had a good look through all my clothes and didn't think much of any of them and she was mean about my shoes too because they came from the wrong shop.

93

"I wouldn't be seen dead in shoes like that," she said, throwing herself onto my bed and waggling her wonderful pink strappy heels in the air.

"Can I try your shoes on, Chloe?" said Amy.
Bella tried them on too.
And even Emily.
"Can *I* try them on, Chloe?" I asked.
"No fear. I don't want your smelly old feet in my shoes," said Chloe.
I wished the dolphin on her T-shirt would swim off with her to the bottom of the sea – and then leave her there, with her head in the sand and her legs in their pink strappy shoes waving in the air.

✳ Fourteen ✳

When we went downstairs – Emily, Bella, Amy and me tip-toeing, Chloe clackety-stomping – Mum and Dad were in the kitchen having *their* tea.

"Are we going to play some more Musical Bumps?" said Amy.

"Boring," said Chloe.

"Are we going to have some more tea?" said Bella.

"Boring," said Chloe.

"Are we going to go in the tent now?" said Emily.

"Boring," said Chloe.

"What would you like to do then, Chloe?" said Mum.

"It's Daisy's birthday. She should choose," said Dad.

"I know!" Mum said quickly.

"Why don't you all go and watch the video Chloe gave Daisy for her birthday? *101 Dalmatians* is a lovely film."

We went into the living room. Chloe carefully shut the door behind us and then slotted the video into our player. We started to watch. It wasn't a lovely film. It wasn't *101 Dalmatians*.

It was another white witchy ghost movie. This one was even worse. It's about a girl walking in the country by herself. She keeps looking round anxiously and you hear these footsteps and then there's this awful waily breathing noise, a bit like Lily having one of her spells but worse, so the girl starts to run and she sees this camping site and she runs harder and shouts but then something grabs at her and you see her face and she screams and screams and screams.

I had to suck my thumb hard to stop myself screaming too.

"Look at little suck-a-thumb! *Baby!*" said Chloe. "She's scared of a silly film."

"I'm scared too," said Emily.

"And me," said Amy.

"Can't we do something else, like see if there's any cake left?" said Bella.

"No, no, you've got to watch the bit that comes next. It's so cool!" said Chloe.

We were at the camping site now. The girl is inside her tent, just waking up and stretching, and then she sees something poking at her tent from the outside and she laughs at first, thinking it's one of her friends. She even calls out to them, but there's no reply, there's just this awful waily noise and then suddenly a terrible white claw rips through the tent and I had to shut my eyes tight and I nearly bit right through my thumb.

"*Watch* it, Daisy. Don't close your eyes!" said Chloe.

"*I* don't want to watch it," said Bella.

"She doesn't have to watch it if she doesn't want to," said Amy.

"Shall we switch it off?" said Emily, getting up.

"Sit down, Emily. You're all babies. Of course we're not switching it off," said Chloe.

But then we heard my Dad calling just outside and Chloe shot up quick and stopped the video. A film on television flashed on instead just in time.

"How are you doing, girls?" said Dad, putting his head round the door. "Are you OK, Daisy?"

"Yes, Dad," I said.

"I thought you were watching *101 Dalmatians*?" said Dad, looking at the television.

"Oh, we *were*. But we just wanted to peek at this film on the telly too," said Chloe in this cutesy-pie tone she uses for her own dad.

My dad didn't look as if he totally believed her. He blinked at the television.

"Well, I don't think you should be watching this old film. I saw it years ago and it gets a bit scary," said Dad.

Compared to Chloe's white witchy ghost films it was about as scary as *Teletubbies*, but I was glad when Dad switched the television off, even so.

"Anyway, I've come to announce that your sleeping quarters are now fully prepared, noble ladies," said Dad in a daft voice, bowing low.

He'd got it beautifully cosy inside the tent, with the big cushions from the sofa to sprawl on and the special garden fairy lights rigged up inside the tent so it glowed precious jewel colours, amber, emerald and ruby. There were lots of our old shawls and rugs and cardis too so that we were still ever so cosy when we were changed into our pyjamas.

Then we talked and talked and talked and talked: about our favourite singers (I copied Emily) and footballers (I copied Emily again) and the boys in our class at school (I didn't need to copy because they're *all* gross). Then we made up our favourite clothes and this time I went first and invented this seriously cool black-and-silver outfit with black high heels and Emily copied *me* because she said she liked the sound of mine so much. We chose our favourite colours (black and silver, naturally) and our favourite animals (Emily and I both said "bears" together and burst out laughing). Then we all said what we wanted to do when we grew up. Emily said she wanted to be a footballer and if she couldn't she'd teach PE in school and *I* said I wanted to be an artist but if I couldn't I'd teach Art in school. Chloe said I was a useless copycat which wasn't fair because I've always loved Art and I'm good at teaching too. I teach Lily lots, even though she doesn't learn very quickly. Chloe said teachers were boring anyway and *she* was going to be a famous actress. Amy said she was going to be a famous dancer and Bella said she was going to be a famous TV chef. Then she said she felt a bit peckish and at that *exact* moment Mum came out with big mugs of hot chocolate (and a hot blackcurrant for Emily) and a bowl of popcorn.

"Wow! This is the best sleepover party ever," said Bella. "Even better than mine."

"It's nowhere near as good as mine," said Chloe.

"We've all had super sleepovers," said Emily. "But yours is just great, Daisy," and she reached for my hand under the rug and gave it a squeeze.

While we sipped our drinks and munched popcorn we swapped our Most Embarrassing

Moments (I'm not going to tell you!) and we laughed so much the bowl tipped over and we had to play hunt the popcorn in our sleeping bags. Then we played Double Dare and some of the dares were amazingly outrageous (I'm not going to tell you again, though I will just say that *one* of us took her pyjamas off and went into the garden and ran right round the tent, but it was dark by then so no-one could see – I hope!)

Then we started to tell ghost stories and that was fun at first but Chloe's started to get a bit too scary.

"Do shut up, Chloe," Emily begged, putting her hands over her ears.

"Don't be stupid. It's just a *story*. Ghosts aren't *real*," said Chloe.

"Yes, they are! My granny kept seeing the ghost of my grandad after he died," said Amy.

"Let's *play* ghosts," said Bella, and she pulled the white pillow case off her pillow and put it over her head and made funny *who-o-o-o* ghost noises. Then she went *oooh* instead because she'd found some more popcorn inside the pillowcase and went gobble gobble munch munch.

"You are a piglet, Bella," said Amy.

So Bella made piglet noises and then we all played a daft game of Farmyard and got the giggles so badly our tummies hurt. Then we sang all the songs we knew and then we played making up a poem together.

I started it.

"We are the special Alphabet Girls."

"Some of us have straight hair, some of us have curls," said Emily.

"We all like to dance if we get the chance," said Amy.

"We eat lots of chocolate yum yum yum," said Bella.

"Chloe and Emily, Amy and Bella, and Daisy Diddums Fat Bum," said Chloe.

"Daisy isn't a bit fat," said Emily.

"*I* am, but I don't care," said Bella. "Daisy, do you think your mum might have some *more* popcorn in the kitchen?"

"I think my mum and dad have gone to bed

now. But tell you what we *have* got . . . my birthday chocolates!"

I handed round the box. Emily said she was far too full up to have even half a chocolate. Amy took one. Chloe chose the special caramel and hazelnut, my favourite. Bella took one – and then another and another – and then even she said sleepily that she was *almost* full up.

We were all starting to feel very, very s-l-e-e-p-y . . .

Bella fell so soundly asleep she started to snore a little bit and we all got the giggles. Then Amy curled up and went quiet. After a long time Chloe dropped off too. Emily and I whispered very, very quietly together. I decided to close my eyes just for a minute and then I was suddenly asleep too . . .

I woke up with a start. I heard this rustling nearby. Then something grabbed hold of my shoulder. The white witchy ghost was coming to get me!

"Help!" I gasped.

"Shut *up*, stupid."

It was only Chloe, wriggling right out of her sleeping bag.

"What are you *doing*, Chloe? It's still the middle of the night."

"I know. I need to go to the loo. You'll have to show me where it is."

"It's upstairs. Mum left the back door ajar so we'd be able to nip in."

"I won't be able to find it in the dark," said Chloe, shaking me. "You'll have to come with me."

"Oooh, I'm so sleepy, Chloe," I said. Then a thought occurred to me that made me wake up properly.

"Hey, you're not *scared* of the dark, are you?"

"Of course not, idiot," said Chloe, but when we crept out of the tent into the black garden a cat suddenly yowled and we *both* squealed and clutched each other. We trekked through the wet grass in our bare feet. We were still holding hands.

"You're shaking, Chloe," I whispered.

"It's cold," Chloe hissed.

It *was* cold. But it was also SCARY. I knew it

was only my scruffy old garden where I played every day, but in the dark it went wild and woody and I didn't like it one bit. I also felt distinctly weird holding Chloe's hand.

As soon as we got in the house we drew apart abruptly.

"Put the light on now!" said Chloe.

"But I'll wake Mum and Dad," I said.

I really meant I'd wake Lily. I shushed Chloe and hoped she'd go quietly. At least she wasn't wearing her clackety-stomp high heels.

But Lily was awake already. She obviously felt it was morning now. She heard Chloe and me padding across the dark landing towards the loo. She felt indignant. She wanted to get up too.

"*UR UR UR UR UR UR!*" Lily wailed.

"A-A-A-A-A-A-H!" Chloe screamed. "It's the witch ghost!"

"What on earth . . . ?" said Mum, stumbling out of her bedroom.

She switched on the landing light. Chloe was crying! And it wasn't just her face that was damp. She'd wet herself!

She gave a little squeak and hurtled into the bathroom sharpish.

"Oh dear," said Mum. "Poor little thing. Look,

you see if you can quieten Lily down while I go and find a spare pair of pyjamas for Chloe. You keep out of the way, Daisy, I expect she'll be a bit embarrassed."

"I'll say!" I muttered.

I went into Lily's room.

"UR UR UR UR UR UR!" said Lily.

"That's right, Lily! You're the greatest. You really frightened her. You're the cleverest sister in the whole wide world."

* Fifteen *

I went back to the tent – but Chloe didn't. When I woke up in the morning she still wasn't there.

"Where's Chloe?" said Emily, leaning up on one elbow.

"Maybe the witchy ghost has got her!" said Amy, rubbing her eyes.

"I wish!" said Bella. She smacked her lips. "Is it breakfast time?"

Mum was pouring juice and laying out bowls of cereal in the kitchen. Dad was eating a banana and looking sleepy. Lily was strapped in her special chair. She sang, "Ur ur ur ur ur," quietly to herself.

There was no sign of Chloe.

"Did Chloe sleep in my bedroom after . . . ?" I said.

"After what?"

"What happened, Daisy?"

"Tell us!"

"Now, now," said Mum. "You don't want to tell tales, Daisy. Chloe decided she wanted to go home so Dad drove her back."

"In the middle of the night," said Dad. "She went all sad and sulky after she wet herself."

"Dad!" said Mum.

"Oops!" said Dad.

"She *wet* herself?" said Amy.

"*Chloe* wet herself!" said Emily.

"And she calls *us* babies?" said Bella.

We had a wonderful time for the rest of the morning, all five of us. Lily kind of joined in too. Amy gave her a drink of milk and Emily fed her some special cereal and Bella crumbled chocolate into very teeny, tiny pieces and spooned them into Lily's mouth. Lily liked all this attention. She particularly liked the chocolate and went, "Ur ur ur ur ur," smacking her lips.

"There. I *knew* she'd like chocolate," said Bella.

Then we all watched television for a bit and then we played this mad game of Charades. Lily played a baby and an old, old lady and we let her be a ghost again too as she was so very good at it. Then Amy's mum came calling for her. Then Bella's dad. Then for a very special half hour it was just Emily and me and Lily. Emily and I rather wanted to play teddy bears but that was right out of the question, so we played hairdressers instead. I styled Emily's hair and she styled mine and then we both styled Lily's hair. I did one side and Emily did the other, plaiting it carefully and arranging her daisy slides. Lily wasn't too sure about this at first but then she got into the swing of it and said, "Ur ur ur ur ur," very happily.

"Oh Lily, you look *lovely*!" said Mum, and she looked like she was going to cry.

"You look utterly gorgeous, little Lily," said Dad, pretending to bow to her. He put his arm round Emily and me. "And you two look ultra-fantastic too."

Emily and I beamed. And then her mum came to collect her. Emily gave me a special big hug and said it had been the best sleepover ever, ever, ever. Then she paused.

"I'm going to break friends with Chloe, Daisy – somehow! So will you be my new best friend?"

"Oh yes *please*, Emily! I'd like that more than anything!" I said.

I was so-o-o-o-o-o-o happy. But I was also a tiny bit scared too, wondering what Chloe would say, worrying what Chloe would *do*.

But you'll never ever guess what! We didn't have to break friends with Chloe. She broke friends with *us*!

When I got to school on Monday morning Chloe was telling a whole gang of girls that she'd been to the worst sleepover party in the world on Saturday.

"Daisy's house is all little and poky and there's no room anywhere and she's got this totally batty, loopy, maniac baby sister who screams all the time." Chloe screwed up her face into a mad leer and wailed. Some of the girls laughed. I clenched my fists.

"You shut up, Chloe. My sister isn't mad. She's got learning difficulties, that's all."

"She isn't Daisy's baby sister, she's her big sister. I like her a lot," said Emily.

"She's special because she's got special needs," said Amy.

"It's sad because she can't do much but she can still eat chocolate," said Bella.

"Why are you all sticking up for Daisy Diddums and her loopy baby sister?" said Chloe, scowling.

"They're not the babies. *You* are," said Emily.

Chloe paused. She went red. She realized we all knew about her little accident. She waited, wondering if we were actually going to come out with it in front of everyone.

We waited too.

"You're not my best friend any more, Emily. You're not my friends either, Amy and Bella. And I wouldn't have *you* for a friend if you were the last girl in the world, Daisy Diddums," said Chloe, and she turned her back on us and went off with this new gang of girls.

It was so-o-o-o-o wonderful! So now Emily and I are best friends and Amy and Bella are best friends and we all go round in a special foursome at school. Chloe doesn't look as if she likes it but there's nothing she can do about it – she knows we could still tell on her.

It's all because of Lily! She's the best sister ever.